Return of
SQUONK

JULIA JARMAN

Illustrated by
JEAN BAYLIS

HEINEMANN·LONDON

For David who wanted to hear
more about Squonk

First published in Great Britain 1995
by William Heinemann Ltd
an imprint of Reed Children's Books
Michelin House
81 Fulham Road
London SW3 6RB

AUCKLAND · MELBOURNE · SINGAPORE · TORONTO

Text copyright © Julia Jarman 1995
Illustrations © Jean Baylis 1995
ISBN 0 434 97239 8

Printed in Great Britain by William Clowes Ltd

A school pack of BANANA BOOKS 73-78 is
available from Heinemann Educational Books
ISBN 0 434 97224 X

Chapter 1

JESSICA DODD WAS worried. She had just said good-bye to Squonk. Squonk was a funny green creature who had come from America – by mistake – in her dad's suitcase. He'd loved living with Jessica. He'd been her best friend until he got homesick. Now Mr Dodd was taking him back to Pennsylvania – secretly – because Squonks aren't allowed on planes. Mr Dodd was going on a business trip and Squonk was travelling in his pocket.

I just hope he stays there, thought Jessica. If anyone sees him …

It was too awful to think about.

I should have gone with him, thought Jessica. He might need help.

Jessica was in the airport shop. Her mum was choosing a book.

The more Jessica thought about Squonk, the more she wished she was with him.

'Don't wanna!' A screaming little girl interrupted Jessica's thoughts.

A stewardess held her hand.

'You've got to come, Sukie.

Your momma's meeting you in
Pennsylvania.'

Pennsylvania – that's where her dad
was going.

That was where Squonk lived!

'No! No!' Sukie shouted.

'It'll be really nice on the plane,' said
the stewardess. 'Now stay with Arnold
and Effie.'

Jessica watched the stewardess taking the three children to Passport Control. She saw Sukie sneak away!

If only I could go in her place, thought Jessica. Then she had an idea! She would stow away!

I know I shouldn't, but Squonk needs me, she said to herself. And I do look a bit like Sukie. We're both wearing blue anoraks. So Jessica tagged on behind Arnold and Effie.

Chapter 2

MRS DODD DIDN'T see Jessica creep away. She was still choosing a book. The stewardess didn't notice Jessica either. She was busy with passports and tickets. The plane was due to leave and she wanted to put the Harrisons on it. Arnold and Effie didn't notice her either. They were too busy arguing.

So Jessica got through Passport Control. She got through the Security Check and into the Departure Lounge, where there was a queue for the plane, and there was her dad near the front!

And there was Squonk peeping out of his flight bag. Oh no! He must have grown too big to fit in Dad's pocket any more. That meant trouble!

When Squonk was happy he grew and when he was sad he cried so much he shrank.

He was happy now, because he was going home, and he was nearly too big for the flight bag!

But nobody saw him get on the plane and Jessica got on the plane too.

She headed straight for the toilets – to hide!

I'll find a seat later, she thought.

Soon she heard worried voices, 'Have you seen Sukie Harrison? We've lost Sukie Harrison.'

She heard Arnold say, 'So what? She's a pain.'

A search began. Someone knocked on the door of the toilets.

'Is that Sukie Harrison in there?'

'No,' said Jessica.

A few minutes later she heard Sukie – and a cross steward.

Sukie had been found in the departure lounge.

'Now sit down you lot and belt up!' said the steward.

Now what? Jessica listened hard. When would it be safe to come out?

She had to keep an eye on Squonk to help him if he got into trouble.

Oh dear. Someone was knocking on the door again.

'Take your seats now, please. We can't take off till everyone is seated.'

Hoping she would find a seat, Jessica opened the door.

And there was a seat! It was behind the Harrisons and a long way from her dad. She could just see him near the front of the plane. Jessica fastened her seat belt and hoped that Squonk was safely asleep in his bag.

Minutes later she was in the air.

Chapter 3

IT WAS GOOD fun! First the stewards showed everyone how to use a life jacket. Then they brought drinks round. Jessica's drink was delicious, but the Harrisons said theirs were horrible. *They* were horrible. The stewards served dinner. Then everyone settled down to watch a film. Everyone except the Horrible Harrisons.

Even when the lights went dim they carried on arguing – about a comic.

'It's mine!' yelled Arnold.

'No! Gimme!' screamed Sukie.

Jessica heard the comic tear.

'Look what you've done!' said Effie.

The steward told them to be quiet – like their sister.

Jessica was wondering what the steward meant, when Arnold shouted.

'What's that?'

'What?' said Effie and Sukie together.

'That green thing!'

Jessica froze.

'It's a frog! It's a frog!' screeched Sukie, climbing on to her seat.

Jessica could see Squonk coming down the aisle.

As Arnold leaped out of his seat, Squonk dived under a seat in the opposite row, and Arnold charged up the aisle.

'Look out everybody! It's under your feet!' he yelled. 'It's a frog, okay! Lift your feet! I'll get it! I'll get it!'

The lights went on and someone screamed. Some passengers bent down to look under their seats.

Looking under her seat, Jessica saw Squonk coming towards her.

She opened her bag – to hide him in – but he hopped across the aisle, into an old lady's knitting bag.

Arnold was close behind.

The steward was close behind him.

He was angry. 'There are no frogs on this plane!'

'What's that then?' said Arnold. He pointed to a wet trail crossing the aisle.

'It's probably where you spilt your drink!' said the steward.

'You lot have been nothing but trouble. Sit down and shut up!'

The Horribles sat down.

'Now,' said the steward, 'I want to hear nothing more about frogs or green things or anything else. I want to hear nothing more from you at all!'

The old lady's knitting bag was getting wetter and wetter.

Jessica leaned towards her.

She was just going to say, 'Excuse me, I've dropped something in your bag,' when someone pushed her aside!

'Gotcha!'

It was Arnold – squeezing a terrified Squonk.

Chapter 4

THE OTHER HORRIBLES were close behind.

'Give it to me. I'm the eldest,' said Effie.

'No me! I'm the youngest!' screeched Sukie.

Arnold squeezed Squonk tightly. 'Finders keepers, that's what I … '

He didn't finish.

'Give that to me.' It was the steward.

'Give that to me.' The steward looked very fierce.

Scowling, Arnold handed Squonk over.

Jessica was frantic. Squonk was so tiny, she thought he might shrink away completely. That can happen to squonks. Now the steward was holding him by one ear. Poor Squonk. He was stiff with fright.

'This is what the trouble's about, is it?' said the steward. 'A toy.'

He glared at Arnold. 'Bit big for this, aren't you?'

Jessica managed to speak. 'It's mine. Arnold took it.'

She held out her hand. 'Please may I have it back? It's my favourite toy.'

The steward looked at Squonk. Then he looked at Jessica.

'Well,' he said, 'you've got better manners than your brother.'

'She's not my sister!' spluttered Arnold, but the steward wasn't listening.

He was giving Squonk to Jessica. 'Take good care of it, my dear. Put it somewhere safe.'

'Thank you,' said Jessica.

Then the steward turned to the others. 'If I hear any more from you, you're for it!' He took them back to their seats. 'Now sit down and BELT UP!'

Jessica heard him as she hurried to the back of the plane. She had to hurry, because Squonk was growing!

In the toilets at last, she closed the door and locked it.

'Wow! That was a close thing! Are you all right?'

Squonk couldn't speak. He just grew and GREW!

Then he hugged her.

'I thought you might need me,' said Jessica.

Squonk hugged her again.

He didn't know what to say.

How brave she was! How clever!

'I just pretended to be with the Horrible Harrisons,' Jessica went on. 'We'll get off the plane the same way. You'll have to shrink though.'

But Squonk grew even more – he was so happy. Then there was a noise outside the door.

'We know you're in there.'

'And we know you've got that green thing.'

It was the Horrible Harrisons.

'We can hear you talking to it. If you don't show us, we'll tell the captain,' said Arnold.

'And the Customs man,' squeaked Sukie.

'And the cops when we get to

America,' said Effie. 'That thing'll be put in a zoo.'

'Or be put down,' jeered Arnold.

Squonk trembled, but Jessica stayed calm.

Then Arnold said, 'We know something else too.'

'Oh?' said Jessica.

'You're a stowaway.'

'You're both stowaways.'

How had they found out? This could mean big trouble.

'So if you don't show us we'll report you – both!'

Jessica thought quickly.

'Can you three keep a secret?'

There was a lot of whispering.

'Well?' said Jessica.

'Sure we can,' said Effie.

'Well then,' said Jessica, 'that green thing, it's not a frog.'

'What is it then?'

'A Martian. So nobody must know,' she went on, 'because it must get back to Pennsylvania to reclaim its spacecraft and call off an invasion of the earth.'

She could hear the Horribles sniggering.

Then Effie said, 'Can we have a look at this er … Martian?'

Jessica could tell they didn't believe her.

'I'll open the door just a little bit,' she said.

And she did.

'Ibble Obble,' said Squonk.

Then Jessica closed the door.

It had been worth it just to see their faces.

Hearing them was even better.

'There's a M-Martian! There's a M-Martian!' stammered Arnold.

'There really is a Martian and he's green and ENORMOUS!' shrieked Effie.

'He speaks M-Martian!' screamed Sukie. 'And he's in there!'

Jessica held her breath. Would the steward come and look in the toilets? She heard his voice.

'That's enough!' he yelled. 'I've had enough of your pranks!'

A few minutes later, there was a public announcement.

'CHILDREN MUST BE KEPT UNDER CONTROL,' said the captain.

'Great,' said Jessica. 'Nobody will believe the Horribles now.'

'Thanks Jessica,' said Squonk. 'You're fantastic.'

Chapter 5

JESSICA WAS VERY worried.

She wanted to put Squonk in her anorak pocket, and go back to her seat, but he was still enormous. He was too big to go through the door. He was too happy, that was the trouble. He was excited about going home.

'You won't get home at this rate,' said Jessica.

That made him shrink a bit, but a few minutes later he grew again.

He said he was thinking about his forest home.

'Well don't think about it,' said Jessica. 'Listen.'

The captain was telling the passengers they were approaching the airport.

Everyone must sit down and fasten their seat belts.

'Home!' said Squonk, growing even bigger.

'You've got to go in my pocket,' said Jessica.

He had to shrink. If they were caught …

It was too awful to think about. What could she do?

Suddenly she said, 'You're a nuisance and I hate you.'

That did it. His eyes filled up.

'Swuff!' Tears flowed down his face – flooding the floor – and he shrank rapidly.

Jessica didn't dare say she didn't mean it. He might grow again. Instead she put him in her pocket, opened the door and rushed to her seat. Then she slipped him into her bag.

Chapter 6

WHEN THE PLANE landed Jessica stayed near the Horribles and they didn't seem to mind.

She saw her dad get off the plane. He looked very worried. He must be wondering where Squonk was.

She followed the Horribles down the steps, across the tarmac into the airport building. Her dad went through Customs. Now she must get through. It was odd. The Horribles were quite nice to her.

'Anything to declare?' said the Customs officer. He hardly glanced at their passports.

'No,' said the Horribles.

'No,' said Jessica, and the Customs man waved them all through.

He didn't even ask to see their bags.
Great so far.

She could see her dad in the crowd.

'Dad!' she shouted, because she
must catch his attention, before he got
in a taxi.

'Dad!'

Jessica started to run after him,
when someone pushed her over – and
grabbed her bag.

She knew who, of course.

He was near the exit whirling her bag above his head.

'Stop thief! Stop him somebody!' she yelled, picking herself up.

Then Jessica ran after him, yelling as loud as she could. 'That boy's got my bag!'

Arnold Harrison was being kissed – by a woman in a leopard skin coat.

She was kissing all the Horribles.

'He's got my bag!' shouted Jessica.

'Liar!' yelled Arnold.

Why didn't anyone help her?

'My Arnie wouldn't steal.' Mrs Harrison kissed Arnold again.

Then Mr Dodd arrived. 'Jessica! What are you doing here?' He was flabbergasted.

'He's got my bag! Get it, Dad!'

Mr Dodd was angry – but with Jessica not Arnold. She tried to grab her bag.

Mr Dodd grabbed her hand.

'Answer me, Jessica!'

'They've got Squonk, Dad!'

The Horribles were getting into a huge purple car.

'He's in my bag! We've got to get him back!'

Mr Dodd took no notice.

'Do you realise what you've done, running away from your mother like that? We must phone her at once,' he said. 'She'll be frantic.'

But Jessica wasn't listening. She was watching the purple car move off.

Arnold Harrison was waving, and squashed in his hand was a tiny miserable Squonk.

Jessica dived into a yellow cab. Mr
Dodd dived in after her.

'Follow that car!' she yelled to the
driver. 'And hurry, please. Drive as fast
as you can!'

'Jessica!' Mr Dodd was furious.

'It's a matter of life and death, Dad!'

There wasn't much time. Squonks
cry when they are sad and when they
cry they shrink. The very sad ones
shrink completely. And Squonk was
very, very sad.

'I told him I hated him. And he
thinks I meant it.' She was very upset.
'He might die, Dad.'

Chapter 7

FORTUNATELY HER DAD seemed to understand. So did the cab driver. He slammed the car into gear and followed the Horribles' purple car. He said it was a Chevrolet, a very fast model.

It headed for the freeway.

There was a speed limit of 40 miles an hour, but the cabbie went much faster. He had to, to keep the Chevrolet in sight.

Jessica could just see Horrible Arnold leering out of the back window – but she couldn't see Squonk. The cab got a bit closer, and Arnold made a very rude sign.

That did it!

The driver accelerated and they shot forward.

The race was on!

Jessica had never travelled so fast in her life.

Seventy miles an hour!

Eighty.

Ninety.

And the speed limit was fifty five!

They passed houses, a garage and a store. They passed a cattle ranch and lots of other vehicles. They passed a big white Mustang, and now the Chevrolet was just in front. The Horribles' faces were pressed against their rear window – and so was Squonk's. Poor thing! He was crying. Could he see her? Jessica waved, hoping he could. The Horribles stuck their tongues out.

Their car turned off the freeway and the road became narrower.

There were traffic lights ahead – red ones!

'We'll get 'em here,' said the cabbie.

But, as the cab screeched to a halt, the Horribles went straight through the lights!

They would never catch up now!

They could see the purple car ahead.
Then the lights turned green.

'Hold tight!' said the cabbie and –
vroom! – the cab was off again!

'We're heading for West
Homestead,' said the cabbie. ''Spect
they live there. If we can just catch
sight of 'em, we'll follow 'em home!'

Straining her eyes, Jessica tried to
see the purple car, but all she could see
were clouds of dust.

Then she heard the sirens.

Speed cops – on motorcycles! Just
like the ones on the telly!

Great, thought Jessica. They're after the Horribles.

But they stopped up the road and waved the cab down.

'You were doing 70 miles an hour,' said one of the cops.

'And that purple Chevrolet ahead's doing 90,' said the cabbie.

'And they have stolen property,' said Jessica.

'What stolen property?' said the cop.

'My daughter's bag,' said Mr Dodd.

'Please catch them,' said Jessica.

The cops zoomed off. Jessica could see their big white helmets weaving in and out of the traffic, as she followed in the cab. Their sirens whined like giant mosquitoes.

'I hope they catch them,' said Jessica.

'They will,' said the cabbie.

And they did!

The cab caught up with them a few minutes later.

Jessica jumped out of the cab as soon as it stopped.

'Hand it over then,' the cop was saying.

'Hand over what?' said Mrs Horrible.

'This little lady's bag.'

'I don't know what you mean,' said Mrs Horrible.

'He does,' said Jessica. She pointed to Arnold.

One of the cops hoiked him out of the car. There was a puddle on the back seat.

'Bit big for that, aren't you?' said the cop staring at Arnold's wet trousers.

Jessica would have laughed if she hadn't been so miserable.

'Now where's this little lady's bag?' said the cop.

It was on the floor. Jessica picked it up.

The bag was very wet.

And there was no Squonk inside.

Chapter 8

'WAS THERE SOMETHING inside?' said the cop.

Jessica didn't know what to say.

'A Squonk,' said her dad.

Fortunately the cop thought Squonk was a toy.

'Have a look in their car, little lady,' said the cop.

The Horribles were on the side of the road. Mrs Horrible was being fined for dangerous driving.

The back seat was very wet. Jessica feared the worst. She couldn't see Squonk anywhere. Mr Dodd put his arm round her.

'Come on, Jess.' He wanted to get back in the cab. 'We really have to phone your mum now.'

The cop had Horrible Arnold by the ear.

'What have you done with the little lady's Squonk?'

'Her what?'

'My green thing,' said Jessica quickly. 'My toy.'

'Oh that,' said Arnold. 'It leaked so I threw it out of the window!'

Chapter 9

'YOU DID WHAT?' said Jessica.

'Where?' said the cop.

'Back there,' said Arnold. He waved his hand in the direction of the freeway.

'I'm real sorry, little lady,' said the cop. 'Your daddy'll buy you a new one I hope. We can't use police time looking for toys, much as we'd like to. We must be off now.'

The cops got on their bikes and roared off.

'Aren't you gonna look for your squonkie?' asked Arnold. 'I threw it out back near that cattle ranch.'

Jessica dived into the Horribles' car. She'd heard something.

'Swuff.'

It was coming from the glove
compartment.

Jessica grabbed hold of the handle –
and pulled it open. And there was
Squonk, tiny but alive!

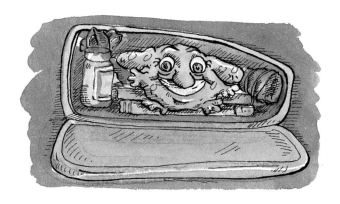

'I love you,' she said, and he leaped
into her arms.

Then he grew.

'SKIDADDLE!' said the enormous
Squonk.

The Horribles left – in a hurry!

'Now we must phone your mum,'
said Mr Dodd.

There was only one thing left to do – take Squonk back to the forest. As they drove there Mr Dodd told Jessica some exciting news. He had a new job – in Pennsylvania!

'So we're coming to live here, Jess. We'll buy a house on the edge of the forest.'

'Will I be able to see Squonk every day?' she asked.

'Yes,' said Mr Dodd.

'That's great,' said Jessica.

'YIPPEE!' said Squonk. 'Come on, I'll show you where I live.'